CW00858838

The Children and the Witches Magic

Pauline Stanley

authorHOUSE®

AuthorHouse™ UK Ltd.
500 Avebury Boulevard
Central Milton Keynes, MK9 2BE
www.authorhouse.co.uk
Phone: 08001974150

Any resemblance to actual places or names is coincidental.

First published by AuthorHouse 4/5/2010

ISBN: 978-1-4490-9544-4 (sc)

This book is printed on acid-free paper.

Dedication

I dedicate this book to Melanie and Michael
thank you for believing in me.

Peter looked through the window to see the arrival of the new nanny, and screamed out " Ahh, she is ugly she looks like a witch she can't stay".

His father George 37, had lost his wife 6 months earlier, and he could not cope with his job and bringing up the children as well so he advertised for a nanny. The children were Peter, who was 12, Julie who was 8 and Steven who was 6.

Peter ran to the children's bedroom and told Julie and Steven of the hag he saw getting out of the taxi. She was horrible she looks like the wicked witch of the west, he told them.

George opened the front door as the bell had rang, and was shocked at the sight of this woman standing on his door step, she was not good looking, George hoped she would not scare the children with her looks.

She told him she had come for the job of a nanny which she had seen advertised in the paper, he let her in and showed her to the drawing room.

She told him her name was Melanie North and she was 35, came from Scotland but had lived in Kent for 10 years. He watched her as she talked she had spiky hair, big bushy eyebrows, a big wide mouth with a faint moustache above it. She had hold of a black case and a black crooked cane walking stick.

She had stopped talking and handed him two references he looked at them, they seemed to be fine they both said they were satisfied with her services, so in desperation he took her on as the nanny to look after his children.

He called the children down to meet the new nanny. The children came running down the stairs in excitement to meet the new nanny.

When they burst into the room they shrieked at the sight of her, " Peter was right she was scary", said Julie to Steven.

George introduced the children to her and told them her name was Nanny North, and they were to be good for her. They didn`t need her, they had been alright on their own for the last six months since their mother had died, thought Peter.

They had the cook to do their meals, and they spent most of the day playing hide and seek in the three acre garden woodland with their play house in the middle.

George showed nanny her room, which was sparse, just a bed, a table and chair, no curtains at the window which was broken, it had no carpet on the floor, there were a few cobwebs in the corner on the ceiling but overall drab, not to worry I can change it into something much more nicer, she thought.

George then showed her the children`s bedroom that was so untidy, she had to step over toys that were all over the floor nearly falling over them.

They walked to the next room, which was a classroom where they had lessons.

He took her back to her room and left her to settle in and un-pack her things, she put them around her to make her feel at home.

She left the room and headed back to the children's classroom, where they were eating their sandwiches. They looked up in shock as she entered the room. She spoke sternly to them saying, "I do not stand for any nonsense, you will do as I say or go to bed with no dinner.

See you in the morning at eight", with that she left the room, the door flew shut with an icy wind.

Well the children didn't want to take orders from an old woman like her. After they had finished their sandwiches, they ran outside to play, forgetting all about nanny's orders for them to start the next day.

When it was starting to get dark, they came home and had something to eat that the cook had made for them, and said goodnight to George before climbing the stairs to bed. They had all worn themselves out, running around the wood, and got into bed and all fell fast asleep.

At 8am, the nanny came in banging a drum, "get up, get up, and get dressed" she shouted, "you have an hour to be ready for your lesson breakfast is on its way, all in the classroom by 9 please children.

With that she went to her room, which was drab and draughty, she lifted up her black cane crooked walking stick and pointed it at the walls as she went round and round in a circle.

The room was transformed into a pretty clean beautiful room with pink curtains at the window, and pink bed spread with a pink carpet on the floor and pink walls, nice work she thought.

9am arrived and she went to the classroom and found it empty the children were certainly mis-behaving. She went to the bedroom but it was empty, she looked out the window to see them all run into the woods, they would have to come in eventually she thought , they will be punished then.

She sat and waited and waited and waited. It was 1pm when she heard their laughter coming in the back door to the kitchen, they ran up the stairs to their bedroom, and all stood quietly as they saw nanny sitting in a rocking chair waiting for them, "you naughty children" she said, "you were supposed to be in the classroom at 9am, you disobeyed me and now you will write 100 lines I WILL DO AS I AM TOLD in your classroom. I want your lines on your desk by 3pm or no dinner".

With that she went out, the door shutting behind her.

Peter took the children to their desks and they started writing their lines.

Steven started crying, his hand was hurting he couldn't do anymore. Peter helped him, and at 2.57pm they had managed to complete their lines just in time as nanny walked through the door. She collected the papers and they could go and get something to eat, and have a few hours playing before bed time.

Peter could not have this horrible nanny telling him what to do anymore. He told Julie and Steven he had a plan, he would run away and his dad would get rid of her.

So he packed a few things and tip toed quietly out of the room, he ran down the stairs to the kitchen and took some bread, then run out the back door into the woods. He did not know where he was going but he just ran and ran. He got to the play house, and went inside to catch his breath, he laid down thinking where to go and before too long had fell fast asleep.

George went up to say good night to the children, and noticed Peter was not in his bed, he asked Julie, she told him Peter had run away as the nanny had punished them by giving them lines to do.

George panicked and ran outside and called for Peter, but no answer.

He ran inside and called the nanny, she came running out of her room, he told her that Peter had run away and it was her fault as she was too strict with them, and he said if he could not find Peter before morning she would be sacked.

She went to her room knowing he would be found, and it was just a game on his part to get her the sack. She smiled.

George ran outside again and called for his son Peter, he ran through the woods calling his name, he had been looking for 2 hours now and it was dark. He ran back to the house to get a torch and went back to the wood and carried on his search.

George was hungry and tired, but wanted to find his son. He came across the play house surely his son would not be there in the dark, so he climbed the ladder and went in. To his amazement he shone the torch around and saw his son asleep on the floor with a blanket over him to keep out the cold.

George bent over and picked him up and carried him down from the play house and took him back to the house. He climbed up the stairs and into his sons bedroom where Julie and Steven were asleep, he crept in and put Peter into bed covered him up and kissed him, words would be said in the morning. He left the room and walked to the stairs, too tired to eat and his hunger had gone, so he turned around and went to his bedroom and got himself into bed and slept till late next morning.

The cook had made him breakfast but he was too late for work to eat it, he would get a snack once he got to work, he ran out the door jumped into his car and sped off down the drive to his work.

Working on his speech as to why he was late, he thought he would speak to Peter when he got home.

8am that morning the bedroom door flew open with a bang, it startled the children who looked and saw it was the nanny and covered the sheets over their faces.

Peter woke and found himself in his bed, and thought he must have dreamt running away, he got up and got Julie and Steven up and washed and dressed, had breakfast at 8.30am and was in the classroom by 9am sharp.

Nanny walked in and was surprised to see the children sitting at their desks, she told them to get their books out and read, and there would be a spelling test and also some sums. They behaved extraordinary good she could not believe they were the same children.

The lesson was over they had done well, they had completed their tasks for the day, she thanked the children and awarded them a merit mark for good behaviour.

George came home from work and summoned nanny to the drawing room. He told her he found Peter in the woods last night, and if it happened again he would have not alternative but to sack her despite what her references said about her.

The next morning after getting dressed and having breakfast they went and sat quietly in the classroom. George came in and had words with Peter, he said he was sorry. George told him he had already had words with nanny and had spoken to her, so to put it behind them and start again. As he was leaving nanny walked in, she made an apology to George and Peter, with that George left for work and left nanny to carry on with the lesson.

The children paid attention to everything that nanny told them. When the lesson was finished she dismissed them, and they went out in the wood to play. She smiled to herself they had behaved and paid attention, they were getting on very well perhaps after the running away of Peter they would be well mannered.

At the end of the day they came in and ran upstairs, they cleaned their teeth and washed, got into their pyjamas and all jumped into bed chattering to each other.

Nanny came in and said what good children they were, the children said "good night" to nanny and as she walked out of the room, the lights dimmed and the door closed behind her.

She went to her room with a snack and raised her black crooked cane walking stick and pointed it around the room in a circle, a glow appeared on the mat, and then a flash. The glow turned into a black cat, it meowed at her and jumped onto her lap and laid down. She carried on reading her book.

George came home from work just in time to say good night to the children before they went to sleep, he asked them if they had been good, they said yes they had done everything nanny had told them.

He went down stairs and got his meal from the cook, and went to his office to sort out his papers.

He felt lonely since his wife died and life was not much fun on his own. He wondered if he would ever meet someone as lovely as his wife. She was a good mother to the children and a good wife to him.

He stopped day dreaming and got on with his paper work. The evening went quickly and it was already 10.30pm so he decided to go to bed, he had had a hard day and knew he would be busy all day tomorrow.

The next day at 8 o'clock, nanny walked into the children's bedroom and expected to find them in bed still, but they were up and dressed and the room was tidy and the toys had been put away. They turned to the door and saw nanny standing there, they said "good morning nanny we will be in the classroom at 9am". They made their beds and went down to the kitchen where cook had prepared their breakfast. They hurriedly ate their breakfast as it was getting close to 9am.

Nanny was in the classroom marking yesterdays lesson when the children went in. They sat at their desks, and nanny started the lesson.

She started on a story of a lonely woman who was so ugly, no one wanted to go out with her. She lived alone and had no friends, her parents were dead, she was alone. The only fun she had was using her magic power, which she had noticed she had when she was young. She could do magic spells like her room and the black cat.

She told the children she wished she was pretty, so she could be married and have a nice house and her own lovely children, with a tear in her eye the children got up from their desk and ran to her throwing their arms around her in sadness, she told them she was too ugly to have a husband as all men had run away from her.

The children said they would help her find a husband. With that said, she pulled herself together and got back to the lesson, and the children returned to their desk and carried on their work.

At 1pm, the children went down to the kitchen for some lunch, and talked over what nanny had told them. "Why couldn't she use her magic to get a husband", Peter said.

Just then Julie heard a miaow, she looked at Peter, "where is that coming from", she said "we don't have a cat", then the door slowly opened and in walked a black cat and purred loudly near the children.

Peter said "it's nannys cat, and it could appear magically when ever it wanted remember, she must have left her room door open, and it got out", said Peter,

"But what did she feed it on", the cook threw it some chicken, which it lapped up, then she put down a saucer of milk for it which it drank.

The children picked up the cat and took it back to nannys room. They were all surprised at the beauty of the room that was not there before.

It was just a dusty old empty room with a glass broken window.

Their dad had put a bed and table and chair in it, it had cobwebs on the ceiling and glass on the floor from the window.

But now it was all clean and neat and pink and pretty. Pink curtains and pink rug, Julie said she wished it was her room.

Peter dropped the cat and said to Julie and Steven, "come on we should not be here it is private, we will be in trouble if nanny catches us in here let`s go". Julie left followed by Steven and Peter shut the door behind him.

They ran out of the house and into the wood they then went to the play house to talk about the day and the story that nanny had told them.

Peter said they should keep it to themselves and not tell dad, so they put their hands in the middle each one piling their hands on top of each other, they had promised. But how would they help nanny get a husband.

She wasn`t very pretty and she had no dress sense, she looked horrible in her black dress and her laced up black shoes, "who would marry her", said Julie.

They got out of the play house and played `I spy`, in the wood. They laughed and screamed when they found each other. They were getting hungry, so started to walk back to the house, that's when they heard a scream.

Peter turned to see Steven caught in brambles, he was crying, and the more he struggled, the more he was getting wrapped up.

Nanny heard Steven scream and looked out of the window to see Peter trying to pull Steven free, but he could not get the bramble off Steven.

Nanny flew down the stairs and out of the house, picking up her black crooked cane walking stick on the way.

She ran to where Peter and Steven were and put her black crooked cane walking stick on the bramble, it wilted to the ground and let Steven walk free.

Poor Peter had thorns in his hands, and they were bleeding, she put her black crooked cane walking stick on his hands, and they magically healed and the thorns all fell to the ground. Peter looked down at his hands and shrieked, he could not believe his hands were not stinging and painful from the thorns.

Peter looked up at nanny, and thanked her. Steven looked up at her and thanked her and so did Julie.

Peter suddenly felt happy she was there, she wasn`t the old hag he thought she was, he hoped she wasn`t.

Peter took hold of Steven`s hand and Julie took the other hand as they followed nanny back to the house.

They went and washed before tea and all met back in the kitchen, where cook was just putting their tea on the plate. "yum, sausage and mash", said Peter, " my favourite".

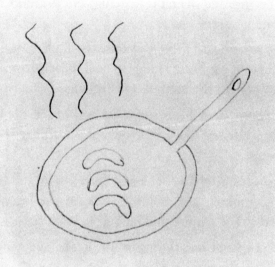

They ate their tea and went to their bedroom and tidied up, then put all their toys on the shelf and in the toy box, the room was neat and tidy.

They cleaned their teeth and got into their pyjamas and jumped into bed.

George got home and went up the stairs to say good night as he always did, he asked them if they had a good day, Peter said it had been an adventure of a day.

Nanny was in her room looking in the mirror, she looked at her ugly face and thought she would try a little magic. She spoke a spell to make her look pretty, and carried on looking in the mirror. She stood there for ages but it never worked so she turned around and sat back in her chair and started reading a book.

George went round and kissed them all good night, he told them how neat and tidy the room was, he walked to the door and left finding it strange not having to step over the toys that normally littered the floor.

He went up to nanny`s room and knocked at the door, it opened and he saw nanny sitting in the chair reading her book.

The rooms magical beauty had gone, is was back to the dusty empty room it was. He walked in and said how happy he was with her and that the children seemed better behaved, they had cleaned up the bedroom and put their toys tidy.

He stared at her, and made himself feel uncomfortable and embarrassed. He felt his cheeks flush as she looked at him, and asked if there was anything else as she would like to retire to bed.

He made his way to the door and said thank you again, stared at her once more and turned and closed the door behind him. She pointed her black crooked cane walking stick at the room, and once again it was back to its pretty pink.

George got his meal and took it in the office and picked at it, thinking of nanny how she had slightly changed, he then shrugged his shoulders and never thought any more about it.

Next morning, after the children had got up dressed, washed and had breakfast, they went to the classroom as usual. But as 9am came, there was no nanny. The clock ticked and ticked and at 10am, Peter got up from his desk and went to her room.

He knocked on the door, but there was no answer, where could she be thought Peter. He opened the door and looked inside, it was all pink and pretty as it was before and the black cat was fast asleep on the bed.

He closed the door and went back to the classroom. He told Julie and Steven that she was not there, they might as well go and play.

They got up and walked out of the room and down the stairs, through the hall and out the front door, all laughing and chattering. They ran through the woods to the play house as it had started to rain. They climbed the stairs to the playhouse and were startled to find nanny in the corner with her back to them, she was crying.

They stood still, nervous and unhappy as it was their place and nanny had intruded in their space. Peter was starting to get angry that she had come in their play house, what was she doing here anyway he thought, why didn't she want to stay in her own room.

He called her name, and as she turned around, he screamed, so Julie screamed, and so did Steven. She was holding a mirror, her moustache had gone. Her eyebrows had grown smaller, her mouth had turned into a pretty smile. She was beautiful and lovely, a completely different nanny.

Her hair was chocolate colour and long and curly, she wore a red dress with matching shoes.

Peter ran to her, "you are beautiful" he said, " what has happened to you nanny, you are so pretty". She couldn't see him properly through her tears. "I don't know" she cried, " I looked in the mirror this morning and I couldn't believe what I was seeing in the mirror".

"Do I really look pretty, you're not just saying that to please me", she said. "No", said Peter, "You are lovely, but what are we going to tell dad when he comes home from work"?

She looked at Peter and said "I will resign from the job, I will tell him tonight".

They all came down from the play house, they were too excited to eat lunch, but couldn't wait till their dad got home from work.

They finally heard the car and rushed upstairs to bed, they quickly got into their pyjamas and they hurried into bed, just before George came up the stairs to say good night.

They wiped the smiles off their faces, and as George walked in, they poked their tired looking faces above the bed sheet.

George said they had been good children and tidied up the bedroom, and hoped they had been good for nanny today. They said they had, so George went round and kissed them all good night, he turned round and went out the door and headed for the stairs.

Meanwhile the children all sat up and giggled to each other, as they knew their dad was in for a shock, which made them laugh even more.

George started to descend the stairs thinking about another boring evening, but if he drowned himself in his paper work, it would take his mind off being lonely.

He went to the kitchen and picked up the meal that the cooked had prepared for him and took it into the office. He started writing out a few cheques to pay the bills he had on the desk, when suddenly, there was a knock on the door, he shouted out to come in. He thought it was the cook asking for money for food, but when he looked up, he fell from his chair.

"Who, who are you? I do not know you young lady, how did you get into my house", he said.

She stood there and cried, reaching for her hankerchief.

"Sir it`s me, nanny North", he came closer and looked at her, "No you can`t be nanny, she was an old ha--- " he didn`t finish the word, but stared at her and looked at her face. He stared into her eyes and realized it was her. With a smile he said "what happened to you"?

"I don`t know sir, I just woke up this morning and looked in the mirror, and couldn`t believe it myself, I would like to resign", she told him.

He looked puzzled and asked her why, she said she was not the woman he had hired for the job. He told her she could stay forever and asked her if she would marry him? She said yes, and he hugged her.

There was an almighty screech as the children burst into the room and ran to their father and nanny, and threw their arms around them.

George looked at Peter and said "did you know about this"? Peter said "yes he had found nanny in the play house crying this morning instead of being in the class room".

George could not take his eyes from nanny, she was beautiful and she was slim and the children loved her.

George didn't go to work the next day he had a wedding to plan.

He went to the vicar and asked him to perform the service in the church, and also to pay someone to put the flowers in the church. He went to the town and bought a suit and clothes for the children and 2 rings, one for nanny and one for him.

He asked his work friend to come and be his best man, and he asked a few neighbours, as he had no family of his own.

The wedding was booked for 2 weeks time.

The day came and George went to the church and to the hall to make sure everything was ready. Then he went home to get himself ready.

Nanny didn't need to go shopping for herself. She waived her black crooked cane walking stick in a circle above her head and from top to toe, it magically transformed her into a beautiful dressed lady.

She wore a satin white dress with a diamond tiara attached to a veil, and white shoes with a big bunch of pink roses.

George was ready and took Julie and Steven to the church. Peter stayed behind to accompany nanny to the church.

Peter went up to her room and knocked on the door, it opened on its own and he walked in to see nanny looking in the mirror.

She turned round and looked at Peter, he was lost for words, she looked beautiful. She asked Peter if she looked okay, he told her she looked lovely.

He then heard the car pull up, it was pink with pink ribbons on it. She bent over to pick up the bottom of her dress, and slowly walked down the stairs, she then walked through the hall and out the front door to get into her car. Peter then followed her holding her bouquet as he held her hand.

They arrived at the church, she carefully got out of the car, and with her arm on Peter's, she walked up the path to the church. When she heard the wedding march she took a deep breath, she smiled at Peter, and walked gracefully up the church aisle towards her future husband.

She looked at Peter and he smiled at her reassuring her that she was fine. They reached the alter and she walked in front of Peter and stood next to George.

The vicar performed the service and they were pronounced man and wife, George turned round and lifted her veil, he gazed at this beautiful lady who was his wife and kissed her.

They all drove to the hall, there was a big cake on the table with a small bride and groom perched on top, a few of the tables were taken with his friends and neighbours, they ate some food and danced and danced and danced.

George stood up and thanked everyone for coming, he then looked at his bride and said how happy he was to be married to the loveliest lady in the world. They all drove back home, and nanny realised some changes would have to be made.

They all arrived home, and the children were so tired that they got on their pyjamas and jumped into bed all excited but exhausted. Julie said how lovely nanny looked, Peter agreed and said how happy his dad looked, they laid there smiling to themselves. Julie looked at Steven who had fallen fast asleep, with that they turned over and both went to sleep.

George was sitting on the sofa with a glass of champagne and his arm around his new bride, they looked back on the day with happiness as everything had gone well and the children had behaved themselves.

As they sat and talked, sipping their drink, Melanie said to George, "what am I going to do about a school teacher, do I carry on, I will be their step mum now". George told her it was up to her, but if she didn't want to carry on he could always hire another nanny, she said she would sleep on it and make a decision in the morning.

She felt nervous about going to bed as she would not be going to her little pink room anymore, but thought it would be a nice room to give to a nanny, should she decide to hire one.

She got up and George followed, putting his champagne glass on the table, he walked towards the door turning the lights off as they made their way up the stairs to bed.

Melanie went straight to the bathroom to clean her teeth and wash, while George went to check on the children, when he returned to the bedroom he saw Melanie in bed, he jumped in and kissed her good night and said thank you for making him the happiest man in the world, they then both went to sleep.

Next morning they awoke to hear the children laughing and shouting,George turned to Melanie and kissed her, he said "what are we going to do about their nanny"? Melanie said she wanted to try and carry on as before, but if it did not work out, she would go back to work and he would have to hire another nanny.

She got out of bed and got washed and dressed, while George got ready for work, then joined her in the bathroom to clean his teeth. She went to the children`s bedroom where they were still shouting and laughing. "Come on children quiet now, lets get washed and dressed and get your breakfast, class starts at 9 o`clock please. The children shouted "oh no, we are not going back to the old routine of things are we"? Melanie sat down and asked them what they wanted, Peter told her "you are our mum now not our nanny, we thought things would be different now". With that Melanie thought it would be better to get another nanny as she thought they would not take any notice of her as a teacher.

She turned and said "come on get dressed, just for this week you can have a few days holiday from the lessons, we can go to the beach today", the children shouted "hoorah", and quickly got washed and run down stairs to the kitchen to have breakfast, where Melanie was preparing a hamper of food to take to the beach.

The children finished their breakfast and ran upstairs to get their swim wear and towels, and ran back down the stairs out the front door and got into the car, waiting for Melanie. She came out the front door struggling with the hamper, Peter jumped out and helped her with it, they put it in the boot and got back in the car and headed off down the drive towards the beach.

They got there after a short drive and all ran out of the car onto the white sandy beach. Melanie took the towels and blankets to sit on from the car and walked to where the children were, she carefully laid out the blankets and put the towels down.

Julie and Steven were splashing about in the water while Peter was making sand castles, he looked over to where Melanie was sitting on the blanket reading a book and went to join her.

"Can I have a drink please nanny", he said, she turned to the bag and gave him a glass of juice, he drank and drank, his thirst quenched. He looked at her again and she looked at him, she caught him staring at her, "what is it Peter", she said, Peter said "we cant go on calling you nanny can we, what do we call you now you are married to dad", she turned and said to Peter "what would you like to call me, after all I am your step mum now", he said "can we call you mum", she smiled and said "of course you can if that is okay with you and the other children", "yes" said Peter, "calling you nanny does not sound right now you are our step mum". She looked at Peter and said "if that is what you want, that is fine with me".

Peter ran off to tell Steven and Julie. They were happy with that. They came running over to her and said they were happy to call her mum, they all sat there on the blanket and laughed. Melanie had acquired 3 adorable well behaved children, they ran off back to the water leaving Melanie to continue her book.

After awhile the children were getting hungry and walked back to Melanie with their buckets full of water and sea shells. She told the children to dry themselves and go up to the car, she picked up the bag with their drinks in and headed back to the car.

She opened the hamper and gave out the food of sandwiches, sausage rolls and crisps, chocolate biscuits and some fruit, they ate and ate till they were full and drank some more juice. They got up then ran back to their buckets on the beach..

Melanie put everything away, picked up her book and went back to the children, she sat there reading while they played with the shells, making patterns in the sand.

As the afternoon went by, it was getting late so Melanie said it was time to go home as their dad would be home soon from work. They packed up and emptied the buckets of water and kept the shells to take home, jumping into the car for the journey home.

They pulled up outside the house, when George turned onto the drive behind them, he pulled up and got out of the car and ran over to Melanie and the children and hugged them. "Had a good day", George said to them, "yes" said Peter, "we have been to the beach". "Dad we want to call Melanie mum, is that okay"? George was surprised, but smiled and felt happy that they had wanted to call her mum, after everything they had been through.

They went to the kitchen and sat down to the meal the cook had prepared for them, sausage and mash, Peter's favourite.

George asked Melanie if she had enjoyed herself, she said yes she had, she had felt part of a happy family and was pleased that the children had wanted to call her mum.

She told George what happened that morning regarding the childrens lessons, and she decided it would be best to get a new nanny. George said okay if that was what she wanted it was fine with him, he would advertise for a nanny tomorrow in the paper, "as long as she was not as bad as you were, when you first started here, she smiled and said "ha ha".

Worn out the children went up the stairs to their bedroom, still chattering about their good day on the beach, Julie had brought some sea shells home and decided to paint them all different colours.

George left the kitchen and made his way to the study, Melanie stayed and helped cook clean up the plates and unload the hamper.

George wrote down the advert he was going to place in the paper and hoped it would be filled as soon as possible, as he had planned a surprise for Melanie. With that done he got up, switched off the light, and went to find Melanie to tell her he was going to bed, as he had an early start tomorrow, she said she would just finish off the tidying up and would join him. He walked up the stairs into the childrens bedroom and kissed them good night, then quietly went to his bed.

By the time Melanie had finished and checked on the children, George was asleep, she tip toed into the bedroom and washed and got into bed, it had been a busy day.

Next morning Geroge placed the ad in the paper and told Melanie to expect a potential nanny to be knocking on the door, kissed her goodbye and left for work.

At 2pm, there was a knock on the door, Melanie went to answer it and was surprised to see an aged lady standing on the doorstep. "Can I help you ", said Melanie, the aged lady said "yes I have come for the job advertised in the paper for a nanny". Melanie invited the lady in and showed her into the living room, as they walked across the hall, Peter was just coming down the stairs to see who it was and looked, eyes wide open, "oh no here we go again", he said and ran back upstairs to the bedroom to tell the others.

Melanie introduced herself and told her the names of the children she hopefully would be caring for. The aged lady told Melanie her name was Miss. Scrubbage, she went into her bag for references and handed them to Melanie who looked over them and nodded, they were excellent.

After a chat, Melanie showed her around the house and took her upstairs to meet the children and see the classroom and where she would be sleeping. As she opened the door to the bedroom, the children jumped to the floor and lined up neatly. Melanie turned to the new nanny and introduced her to the children, Peter and steven bowed and Julie curtseyed, Miss Scrubbage said she was pleased to meet such well behaved children and hoped she would be looking after them soon, with a gleam in her eye. Melanie opened the door for her and they both left the room and went back downstairs. The children all whispered and Peter thought she looked a nice old lady.

They heard the front door close and ran downstairs to talk to Melanie,

She told them she would start in the morning and hoped they got along with her and behaved themselves.

Next morning came and at 7.30 there was a knock on the front door, George opened it and saw this aged lady standing on the doorstep, "hello" he said, "you must be Miss Scrubbage please do come in".

George asked her if she knew what she had been told to do that day as he was in a rush to get to the airport, he was taking his wife on a honeymoon week-end, she said she did know, with that he ran upstairs to Melanie and told her the new nanny was here, and he had a wonderful surprise , he was taking her to Paris for a short honeymoon and could she hurry up and get packed the plane was leaving in 2 hours. She could not believe it, and smiled at George and kissed him. She got out her case and packed a few things and ran down the stairs where George was waiting.

They bid farewell to Miss Scrubbage saying they would be back in a few days and ran out of the front door to the waiting taxi.

The new nanny hung up her coat and bag, taking a cane and some papers from it, she thudded up the stairs to the bedroom where she threw open the door with a bang, the children got up quick to see what was happening, and saw her standing in the door way.

Now you horrible little brats you are in my charge now, get up, dress and have some breakfast, I shall see you in the classroom at 8.30am.

She walked to the classroom and put the papers on the desks. At 8.30, the children walked in and sat at their desks looking through the papers, she slammed the door shut and turned the key to lock it. She walked up and down the classroom slappping the cane down on her hands, telling the children what was expected of them.

She said if they behaved badly in there they would feel the slap of her cane and she slapped it down swiftly on the edge of Peter's desk with a 'whoosh', it made Peter jump up with fright. She told them to fill in the papers she had left them on their desks. Peter read through them and realised they were tests, some questions were really hard to do, they carried out her wishes.

As the hours ticked by the children were having problems doing the tests.

Peter asked if they could stop as it was lunchtime, she turned to him, her eyes turning red and snarled, "you finish these papers first my boy or you will feel the slap of my cane across your hand". Peter was angry, Melanie was not as horrible as her, he thought.

She walked over to Steven who had fallen asleep, she slapped his arm with her cane, "wake up boy, get writing, I do not care if it takes all day you will finish these papers.

Peter felt trapped how could he escape she had locked the door, he decided he did not like her, and she had a funny name.

Time went by and it was nearly tea time, she looked at the papers, they still had not finished, she walked over to the door and unlocked it and said "you may go but you will be punished for not finishing your papers". They run out and went to the bedroom a bit tired, but not hungry.

Julie said she did not like her she was horrible, nanny was just walking by the door and heard Julie, she walked straight up to her and slapped her cane across her hands, "do not talk about me behind my back you naughty child, you will get double punishment tomorrow".

Julie started to cry, "I hate you", she screamed. "Get up you little brat and get back to the classroom, Julie walked back and sat at her desk, the nanny removed the key and locked her in. Julie ran to the door screaming "let me out, let me out". Peter and Steven ran to the classroom and shouted at nanny to let her out, nanny unlocked the door and opened it, Peter thought she was going to let Julie out but instead she pushed Peter and Steven in and re-locked the door. "When you have thought about what bad dis-obedient brats you have been, I will let you out".

Peter opened the window and saw a way down, they could climb down the trellis and run to the playhouse and stay there till mum and dad came home. They quietly climbed out the window and down the trellis until they were all safely on the ground, they ran to the kitchen and got some food and drink and ran back to the playhouse.

After 2 hours, the nanny went to unlock the classroom, they should have thought about their behaviour by now, she thought. She opened the door and found the room empty. She flew into a rage, and screamed, she ran to the open window and looked out, "wait till I find you ", she screamed, "you horrible brats".

The children heard her screams and were scared of the thought of what she would do to them if she caught them. They ate and ate as they were starving, Peter said "wait till dad comes back with our new mum, I will tell them what she has done to us.

He turned and heard footsteps coming up the steps to the playhouse. Peter put both arms around Julie and Steven, as the door opened nanny was standing there with her cane. "Why you horrible brats, get out, get out", she shouted, and marched them off to the cellar and locked the door behind them.

It was dark and dusty and had mice running everywhere, cobwebs hung all over the ceiling, Julie and Steven were crying, they wanted their parents to rescue them from the wicked old nanny.

"Don`t cry", said Peter, lets look for a way out, Julie dried her eyes and started looking around the cellar. It was very dark, she screamed as a mouse ran over her feet.

Peter grabbed her hand and she grabbed Steven's hand and they walked around together.

Peter thought, she can't leave us down here all night. He looked around for a torch and found one in a chest of drawers. He shone it around, there was an old bed, some rusty bikes the children had when they were younger, a kitchen table and a sofa that was covered with plastic sheet.

Peter pulled the sheet off and they sat down, Steven started to cry and was soon joined by Julie. Julie sobbed to Peter "how long will she leave us down here, suppose she never lets us out". Peter looked at his watch it was 7.30pm, they would have been getting ready to go to bed, instead they were locked in a dirty cellar, with no food or drink.

Just then he heard the door open, he heard plates being put on the stairs, "here brats have something to eat, you will need your strength tomorrow". The door closed and was locked again, they went up the stairs to find 3 plates of stew, they picked up the plates and took them back down into the cellar. Peter shone the torch on the plates, it was green stew. "Don't eat it, It might be poisoned" Peter said. Julie said "she wouldn't poison us would she".

Peter put the plates on the floor, and a few of the mice were interested in it, they began eating it. Soon there were about 5 mice all eating the green stew.

Peter carried on looking around with the torch, he let out a yelp. "Julie come quick", she got up and ran to where the torch was shining, "what is it Peter" she said, he shone the torch up the wall to a window, but it was too high for them to reach.

Julie noticed the mice that had eaten the green stew were asleep on the floor, she called Peter, he shone his torch on the mice but noticed they were still breathing. "They are unconscious" he said, "they have been drugged". Julie panicked, "what are we going to do, suppose we get drugged, what will she do with us Peter". He told her not to think like that, they will get out some how. Peter was scared, he hoped they would find a way out, and what was in that stew to make it green he thought, yuk.

Peter had an idea, he look at the table, then the window. "Julie help me push that table over here, perhaps I can reach it if I stand on the table".

She started pushing it, but it was a little too heavy, "Steven come over here and help me", she called. He pushed as hard as he could with Julie and it moved to the wall, Peter stood on the table but could still not reach.

"Julie find me something to stand on", he said, she looked around and found a small crate, she got Steven to help her carry it over to Peter. They pushed it onto the table, Peter stood on it and found he could reach the window.

It would not open, it was stuck. He jumped down and looked for some tools, as the window had iron bars over the glass, he could break the glass and climb through.

He looked in the chest of drawers and found some tools in the bottom drawer, there was a big hammer and a screwdriver, another torch and some pliers and a length of rope.

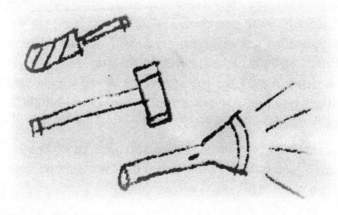

He grabbed the hammer and climbed back on the crate and hit the window with the hammer, he hit it and hit it and hit it, suddenly the window flew open. He looked down it was a long way down to the ground, he climbed back down from the table, he needed a length of rope.

He picked up the rope and tied it to the bars and threw it out of the window. He told Julie and Steven to climb on the table, he picked Steven up and sat him on the window sill. He told him to hold the rope and carefully lower himself down to the ground and stay there and wait for him and Julie, he did it. Julie was next, she grabbed the rope and slid down to the ground and put her arms around Steven while they waited for Peter to join them. He carefully climbed out the window and slid down the rope and joined Julie and Steven safely on the ground.

They ran to the playhouse, they had crisps and biscuits to eat and a bottle of juice to drink. Peter wondered what to do, dare he walk back to the house and phone for the police or would he get caught again. He was too scared to think of it, but thought it would be better than staying here, or would it, they had food, they only had a day before George and Melanie came back.

They laid down and fell asleep, exhausted.

Peter woke up with a start, he looked around and saw Julie and Steven still asleep. Looking out of the playhouse it was morning, he looked at his watch it was 8.30am, he woke Julie and Steven.

Just then he heard a car enter the drive, they all got down from the playhouse and ran to the drive. "It's mum and dad", said Peter, he ran over to the car with Julie and Steven following him. Melanie saw them and was shocked at the dirty clothes they were in, she threw her arms open and cuddled them.

"What is the matter", she said when she saw Julie and Steven cry. Peter told her what the new nanny had done to them, and asked her where his dad was as she was alone. "He had to wait for the luggage, it was put on the wrong plane, he had to wait for the other plane to land", she told Peter.

Melanie was very annoyed to hear what had happened to the children. She ran up to and opened the front door just as the new nanny was coming up the stairs from the cellar, "you horrible brats" she yelled, "wait till I get hold of you".

When she got to the top of the stairs she froze, as the person she saw at the door was Melanie. "Oh hello mam, I have been playing with the children", she said. "No you have not" said Melanie, "I heard all about what you have done to my children locking them in the cellar, don't you know we have mice down there, that is no place for children".

Melanie took her black crooked cane walking stick and pointed it at the new nanny, and said "kiru kiru carlu stibu", with that all stars appeared around the new nanny and before she could realise what was happening to her, there was a puff of smoke and she had disappeared and turned into a brown mouse, it scuttled off down the cellar. Peter ran over and locked the cellar door, saying "now you can be locked in forever", he turned to Melanie and put his arms around her, "you saved us mum, you saved us".

"I am so sorry children", she said, "I shall never leave you again and no more nannies. She looked and saw a taxi coming up the drive with George and the luggage in it, he ran to his new family and hugged them all.

THE END

Lightning Source UK Ltd.
Milton Keynes UK
06 July 2010
156602UK00001B/23/P